Rainbow Swirl

READ ALL THE CANDY FAIRIES BOOKS!

Chocolate Dreams

COMING SOON:

Caramel Moon

Candy Fairies

Rainbow Swirl

HELEN PERELMAN

ILLUSTRATED BY
ERICA-JANE WATERS

ALADDIN
NEW YORK   LONDON   TORONTO   SYDNEY

This book is a work of fiction. Any references to historical events, real people, or real locales are used fictitiously. Other names, characters, places, and incidents are the product of the author's imagination, and any resemblance to actual events or locales or persons, living or dead, is entirely coincidental.

ALADDIN

An imprint of Simon & Schuster Children's Publishing Division

1230 Avenue of the Americas, New York, NY 10020

First Aladdin paperback edition January 2010

Text copyright © 2010 by Helen Perelman

Illustrations copyright © 2010 by Erica-Jane Waters

All rights reserved, including the right of reproduction in whole or in part in any form.

ALADDIN is a trademark of Simon & Schuster, Inc., and related logo is a registered trademark of Simon & Schuster, Inc.

For information about special discounts for bulk purchases, please contact Simon & Schuster Special Sales at 1-866-506-1949 or business@simonandschuster.com.

The Simon & Schuster Speakers Bureau can bring authors to your live event.

For more information or to book an event contact the Simon & Schuster Speakers Bureau at 1-866-248-3049 or visit our website at www.simonspeakers.com.

Designed by Karin Paprocki

The text of this book was set in Berthold Baskerville Book.

Manufactured in the United States of America

0213 OFF

8 10 9 7

Library of Congress Control Number 2009019981

ISBN 978-1-4169-9455-8

ISBN 978-1-4169-9870-9 (eBook)

For Emily Lawrence,

an editor sure as sugar!

Contents

Rainbow Swirl

CHAPTER
1

Gummy Dreams

Raina, a Gummy Fairy, grinned as she flew over Gummy Forest. Sweet, fruity smells filled the air as she glided down into the forest. She loved the colorful gummy trees and gummy wildflowers that filled her home. From the sky above, the forest was a beautiful rainbow patchwork.

"Lunchtime!" Raina sang out. She swooped down to Gummy Lake in the middle of the forest.

Raina was in charge of taking care of the gummy animals. All of the animals, from the adorable gummy bears to the mischievous gummy fish, loved her. Her kind and patient nature made her perfect for the job.

"Come and eat," Raina called. She flew over Gummy Lake, sprinkling flavor flakes in the water for the fish.

A swarm of bright red, green, yellow, and orange gummy fish surfaced and gobbled up the food.

Every day at the same time Raina would give the gummy fish their flavor flakes. The Fairy Code stated that gummy fish needed one

serving of flavoring a day. Raina had memorized the Fairy Code Book. Some of her fairy friends made fun of her for following the rules so closely. Berry, a Fruit Fairy, and Dash, a Mint Fairy, were not big on following codes and rules. But Raina liked order and rules.

After giving the gummy fish their lunch, Raina poured the rest of the flavor flakes into a hollowed-out gummy log for the gummy bears. Then she poured in some sweet syrup to make a sticky mixture. She rubbed her hands on her dress. A few more flavor flakes stuck on her dress wouldn't matter. Her dress already had every color of the rainbow!

Raina was named after the Great Rainbow that appeared the day she was born. Because she was born under the rainbow, she loved bright colors—which was part of the reason she loved Gummy Forest so much.

She blew a few notes on her red candy whistle, and the little gummy bears came out of their caves. The cheerful little bears all lined up at the tree to get a scoop of their sticky treat. Raina made extra sure their food mixture was as sweet as honey.

The bears all reached out their paws to get their share. A little red bear slurped down his portion quickly.

"Slowly," Raina said gently. She patted the little red cub on the head. "Nokie, I know that you're hungry, but there's plenty here."

The red bear took his scoop and then waddled over to the gummy tree to lick his paws.

Raina smiled at the line of cute bears. Of all the gummy animals, she liked the gummy bear cubs the best. With their plump bellies and jolly personalities, the bears were fun to be around. Especially little Nokie.

Raina looked over at the tree behind her to see the young cub eating. Nokie was always first in line for feedings. Raina smiled at the bright red cub. Then she tucked her long, straight dark hair behind her ears and began to scoop out the food for each of the bears.

"Hi, Raina!" Berry called out. The Fruit Fairy flew down through the gummy trees and landed next to her friend. "I thought I would find you here." She pointed to the line of bears. "I see it's feeding time," she said, smiling. Berry liked the gummy cubs too.

"Right on schedule," Raina replied happily. She grinned at the beautiful Fruit Fairy. Berry's raspberry-colored dress wasn't stained or creased, like Raina's dress. And sparkly sugarcoated fruit-chew clips held her hair in a perfect bun. Berry always looked her best.

"What brings you to Gummy Forest?" Raina asked.

Berry reached into the bag that was slung around her shoulder. "I am delivering some fresh strawberry syrup," she replied. She held out a jar. When the sun hit it, the red liquid inside glowed. "I just made the syrup this morning. It's *berry* fresh," she said, giggling.

"Perfect," Raina replied. "I'm sure Miro will be happy to have that. She's over by the gummy flower patch." She pointed to the young Gummy Fairy watering a bunch of seedlings. "She'll be glad to get the new flavor for the flower garden."

"Thanks," Berry said. She put the jar back in her bag for safekeeping.

When the last gummy bear had his serving, Berry helped Raina clean up. Together, they carried the gummy bears' feeding log over to the lake to wash it.

"Have you decided what you are going to make for Candy Fair this year?" Berry asked as she scrubbed the inside of the log clean.

Raina nodded her head quickly. Candy Fair was all she had been thinking about! She had been doing research, trying to find just the right new candy to make for the fair.

"I want to make a new candy," Raina replied. "Something extraordinary!"

Candy Fair was a spring event that was held every four years at the Candy Castle. All the

fairies throughout Sugar Valley displayed their candy in the Royal Gardens. White tents were set up, and each fairy had a booth to show her candy. Fairy Princess Lolli was the fairy who ruled over Candy Kingdom, and she sampled all the candy. The princess and her Royal Fairy advisers gave the fairy with the best candy the honor of the sugar medal. They had a difficult job, but they each had a very good sense of taste and were extremely fair.

This year Raina wanted that medal more than anything. It would be the first year that she was competing. Four years ago she was not old enough. But this year was a different story. This year she not only wanted to show candy, she wanted to win.

Raina had another reason for wanting to win

 10

so badly. No Gummy Fairy had ever won the sugar medal. In all the books that Raina had read, she couldn't find one time that a Gummy Fairy had received the first-place honor. The medal usually went to a Chocolate Fairy, and there were a few years that other fairies had won. But never a Gummy Fairy. This seemed unfair to Raina. This year Raina vowed to make the outcome of Candy Fair different.

"I want to be the first Gummy Fairy to win the sugar medal!" Raina exclaimed. She grinned at her friend. She hoped her dream of winning would come true. "What about you? Have you decided what you are going to make?"

Berry spread her pink wings. "I'm not sure," she said. She looked down at her sparkly shoes. "We'll see."

"We always said that we'd all make candy for the fair," Raina said. She shook her head in disbelief. "How could you not make something?" she asked.

Berry looked down at the ground. She didn't answer Raina's question. She didn't have the right words. She knew how Raina felt about Candy Fair. The problem was that she didn't feel the same way.

Berry lifted up the end of the log and placed it on the ground. "So what are you going to make?" she asked, changing the subject. "You need to decide soon."

"I'm still doing research," Raina said. "But you can be sure as sugar that this year a Gummy Fairy is going to win Candy Fair!"

CHAPTER

2

Sun Dip Treats

A few days later Raina flew quickly toward Red Licorice Lake. The large yellow sun was beginning to dip below the Frosted Mountains. Raina couldn't wait to see her friends. She was excited about a new gummy candy she had grown. She was carrying a sample of her new candy to Sun Dip.

Sun Dip was a time for all the fairies to nibble on candy and rejoice in another day in Sugar Valley. And maybe today try a new gummy candy that would win first prize at Candy Fair. Raina hoped her friends would like the new sweet treat.

The sky was full of swirls of orange, pink, and a touch of lavender. Sun Dip was Raina's favorite time of day. All the scents in Sugar Valley were the strongest in the early evening. The gentle winds blew sweet smells from all areas of the valley. Sun Dip was the perfect time for fairies to come together and visit. Work was done for the day, and all the fairies enjoyed the quiet time with their friends.

Raina and her friends gathered at the hill on Lollipop Landing near Fruit Chew Meadow.

On the hill the friends could sit and watch the sun dip below the mountains. Between the colorful lollipops and the rolling meadow full of fruit chews, the area was a favorite spot for the friends.

"Hi, Raina!" Melli called out, waving to her. The Caramel Fairy was sitting on a large, round purple fruit chew.

"Hi," Raina said. She landed next to her friend and held out her basket. She couldn't wait for Melli to have a taste.

"Oh, what did you bring?" Melli asked. She looked into the basket.

"Try some of my new gummy berries," Raina told her. She took the cloth off her basket to show Melli. The basket was full of all different colors of strawberry-shaped gummy berries.

"You grew these?" Melli said, and gasped. "Raina, these look sensational. I've never seen so many different colors of berries."

"Taste one," Raina said. "I hope you'll like them." She handed Melli a bright blue berry.

As soon as Melli popped the berry in her mouth, her eyes grew wide. "Sweet sugar!" she cried. "This is delicious!"

Raina beamed with pride. She knew the strawberry-shaped candy looked pretty. But in order to win the sugar medal, the candy had to taste good too.

"Is this what you are going to show at Candy Fair?" Melli asked. "They look like strawberries, but they don't taste like strawberries. And so many colors! This one was very tasty."

"Thank you," Raina said. "I've been

researching, and I can't find any other gummy berries in the Fairy Code Book." She pulled a stack of books from her bag. "Actually, I haven't been able to find any gummy berries in any of these books."

Melli glanced at the pile of books in front of Raina. She kept pulling more and more books out of her bag: *Fairy Foods*, *The Joy of Sugar*, *Gummy Gigi's Treats*, and *Berry Delicious Sweets*.

"You've certainly done your research," Melli said, nodding her head. She stared at the tall stack of books in front of Raina.

"Where's Cocoa?" Raina asked. She looked around for the Chocolate Fairy.

Cocoa the Chocolate Fairy would never sugarcoat the truth. If she didn't like the candy, she would tell Raina.

 17

"Right behind you," Cocoa said, laughing. She tapped Raina on the shoulder.

Raina should have known that wherever Melli was, Cocoa wasn't far behind. The two fairies were always together.

"Hi, Cocoa," Raina said. She loved Cocoa's long dark curls. Her own dark hair was just as long, but it was stick straight.

Cocoa peered inside Raina's basket. "What did you bring?" she asked. "Gummy berries?"

"Yes, they are all different-flavored berries. I changed strawberries into flavored gummy berries!" Raina declared.

"She's going to show them at Candy Fair," Melli added.

"Chocolate sprinkles, Raina!" Cocoa exclaimed. "Melli and I haven't even thought of

what we're going to do yet. And you already have your candy!"

"Well, I've been trying out some new things," Raina confessed. She held out the basket to her friend. "Try one."

Raina waited as Cocoa popped one in her mouth. She watched as Cocoa swished the candy around her mouth and then swallowed.

"Well?" Raina asked. She couldn't stand waiting!

"Choc-o-rific!" Cocoa shouted.

Fluttering her red wings, Raina raised her feet off the ground. "Really? You like them?"

Cocoa nodded her head. "Good work," she said. "Did you find these in one of your books?"

"No," Raina said. "I wanted to make sure no one had ever created these candies before. The best chance for the sugar medal is to come up with something totally new."

Melli and Cocoa shared a look. When Raina got focused on a task, she had a one-track fairy mind.

"Hello, fairies," Dash greeted her friends. Most Mint Fairies were small, but Dash was the smallest in Sugar Valley. Though she was tiny, she had a big personality—and appetite. She straightened her white dress and settled down to snack on some of Cocoa's chocolate squares.

"Slow down," Cocoa said, laughing. "I brought those for everyone to share."

Dash giggled. "Sorry!" she said. She licked her fingers. "These are my favorites, you know."

"Dash, you say that about every candy!" Melli said, smiling. Then she noticed a small rip

21

in Dash's dress. "Dash, what happened to your dress?" she asked.

"Oh, it's nothing," Dash said. She fluttered her silver wings. "I just got it caught when I was testing out my new sled."

"Sled?" Cocoa asked. "It's springtime, Dash! Haven't you noticed?"

"Winter is a long time away," Raina added.

Dash shrugged. She loved marshmallow sledding. She had won the Sugar Valley sledding competition two years in a row. Winter couldn't come fast enough for her.

"Yum, what are those?" Dash asked. She peered inside Raina's basket of gummy berries.

"Try one," Raina said. She held the basket up for Dash to take a berry.

"Holy peppermint!" Dash cried after she

ate one. "These are yummy. Where'd you find them?"

Spreading her wings proudly, Raina smiled. "I grew them especially for Candy Fair."

"Nice job," Dash said, reaching for another.

Raina looked up in the sky. "Where's Berry?" she asked. "I wanted her to try one."

Usually Berry was the last fairy to arrive since she took the longest to get ready. But the sun was already down. Sun Dip would be over very soon.

"I'm sure she'll be here soon," Melli said. She put her hand on Raina's shoulder. "You know Berry is always late."

23

"Can I have another one of those berries?" Dash asked.

Raina smiled. She held out her basket. She was feeling good about her candy, but she wanted one more opinion. She looked to the sunset sky, hoping to see Berry . . . soon.

CHAPTER 3

Candy Spirit

I see Berry," Raina said, squinting. She pointed up in the darkening sky.

"I wonder what she's got in her basket?" Dash asked, looking up. "Maybe she has a new candy for the fair too."

"Oh, Dash," Melli said, laughing.

"Or maybe she's bringing some fruit leather!"

Dash said excitedly. She jumped to her feet. Her large blue eyes were sparkling. "Those are my favorite."

Melli, Cocoa, and Raina all laughed. Every candy was Dash's favorite.

"Hi, everyone," Berry said cheerfully. "I've got to show you these amazing fruit chews." Before she even landed on her feet, she was showing off her sparkling candy jewels. "This new crop is the best ever. Look at these!"

"Oh, Berry," Melli said, looking at the candy. "These are beautiful. You're right. These are all supersparkly."

"Are you going to show those at Candy Fair this year?" Raina asked.

Berry started to laugh. "Sweet sugar!" she cried. "These are not for eating." She scooped up the candy and placed the jewels back in her basket. "These are going to be the jewels in my new necklace."

"I don't know," Dash said, looking over. "They look good enough to eat."

Berry rolled her eyes, and then a smile spread across her face. "Everything looks good enough for *you* to eat, Dash!"

"I'm serious," Raina said. "The rules of Candy Fair aren't only about the best-tasting candy. You can get an honorable mention for color and shape as well."

"Leave it to Raina to know *all* the rules of Candy Fair," Cocoa said. She sat down on a hard candy rock and took a sip of sugar nectar from a nearby flower.

"It's true," Raina told her friends. She folded

her arms across her chest. "The candy just needs to be created by a fairy." She grinned at Berry. "I think you should show these at the fair. Everyone will love them."

Berry flapped her wings and sat down on the red sprinkle sand. "I'll think about it," she said. She sighed heavily. "I'm not sure I'm going to show anything at the fair."

"What?" Raina said. She couldn't believe her ears. "What do you mean, you're not going to show candy at the fair? It's all we've talked about for the past four years! It's everyone's dream to win the sugar medal at Candy Fair!"

Berry shrugged. She looked down at her toes. "It's all *you've* talked about," she said softly. "It's *your* dream." Then she picked up some sprinkles in her hand and let the tiny grains fall through

 28

her fingers. "I'm just not sure that I want to compete. I've been busy with my jewelry."

"Melli and I are going to work together," Cocoa said, stepping between them. "We're going to do a caramel and chocolate candy." She turned and fluttered her wings with Melli.

"What about you, Dash?" Melli asked. "I'm sure you have some minty surprise blooming."

Dash shook her head. "No, I haven't had time. I'm too busy building a new sled for the marshmallow slopes."

"What's in your basket, Raina?" Berry asked. She pointed to the basket next to her friend.

Raina had almost forgotten to ask Berry to try her new candy. She held out the basket. "These are my new gummy berries for Candy Fair," she told her.

"May I try one? They look good," Berry said.

As she handed the candy to Berry, Raina couldn't help but feel a swirl of sadness surround her.

She couldn't understand how Berry and Dash didn't want to compete. She had thought all her friends were just as excited as she was about the upcoming candy event. Didn't they have the candy spirit too? She never imagined going to the fair without all her friends. Suddenly, going to Candy Fair didn't seem as sweet to her. . . .

Melli noticed the sad look on Raina's face. "Don't worry, Raina," Melli said. She came over to her and put her arm around her. "Cocoa and I are going to the sign-up for the fair tomorrow

at Candy Castle. Why don't we meet up and go together?"

Raina smiled, thankful for Melli's excitement. "Yes," she said. "Let's get there early. I want to make sure to be one of the first fairies to sign up for the fair."

"That's the spirit," Cocoa said, jumping up.

"These gummy berries are scrumptious," Berry said. She reached for another one from Raina's basket. "And I love how colorful the sweets are. You have a berry flavor for every color of the rainbow!"

Raina smiled. Berry had noticed the one thing she was most proud of. Maybe her candy really could win the sugar medal! She spread her wings. Suddenly she had even more candy spirit bubbling up inside of her. Even though she was disappointed that Berry and Dash were not competing, she had to focus. She'd have to concentrate if she was going to win . . . with or without her friends.

Sweet Sign-up

Raina set out for the Royal Gardens very early the next morning. The sun was just rising over the pink-and-white Candy Castle, and all of Sugar Valley was still. To Raina, the air smelled especially good this spring morning. Springtime was her favorite season in Sugar Valley. So many of the candy trees, bushes, and flowers were in bloom. Even the lollipop trees had sprouted by the royal gates, making the entrance to the castle more grand than on a normal day. With more candy in bloom and the added decoration, the castle looked ready for Candy Fair. Raina sighed as she took a deep breath. She had been waiting for this for four long years!

She waved when she spotted Melli and Cocoa just outside the royal gates. But much to Raina's surprise, the three of them weren't the first fairies there.

"Sour sticks!" Raina cried. She saw the long line of fairies waiting. "I thought we'd be the first fairies here!"

Melli flew up right behind her. "This isn't a race, Raina," she said. She put her hand on Raina's shoulder. "Besides, the line isn't that long."

 36

"I suppose," Raina said, looking around. She looked up at the sky. "I guess Berry and Dash really aren't going to come after all," she said sadly.

"Just because they aren't showing candy this year doesn't mean they won't come to the fair," Melli told her.

"I know," Raina said, brushing her foot on the ground. "I just hope they'll change their minds."

"Maybe," Cocoa said. She looked toward the Candy Castle. "I wonder if Princess Lolli is here," she said.

Princess Lolli and Cocoa had recently gone on a journey over the Frosted Mountains to Black Licorice Swamp. Mogu, the sour old troll who lived there, had stolen Cocoa's chocolate eggs. The two fairies took a dangerous journey to see him. Since that time, Cocoa and Princess Lolli had shared a special bond.

"Of course she's here!" Raina replied. "How could she not be here for Candy Fair sign-up? Candy Fair is the most important candy event."

Cocoa shrugged. "Not to every Candy Fairy," she said.

Raina's eyes opened wide. "What are you talking about?" she said. "Candy Fair is one of the greatest candy events. Besides, it's a huge honor. Every fairy knows that Princess Lolli decides who gets the sugar medal. "

"Princess Lolli *and* her royal advisers," Melli added.

Raina felt her face getting red. Why weren't her friends taking this event more seriously? Didn't they realize the importance of the fair?

"You don't have to get your wings in a flutter," Cocoa told her. "I was just saying . . ."

Melli stepped in between her friends. "Look, we're next in line," she said cheerfully. "You see, the wait wasn't long after all."

The three fairies moved up closer to the middle of the garden. There was a long white table set up between the rows of chocolate oaks. Tula, a trusted Royal Fairy adviser to Princess Lolli, was writing down on a giant scroll the name of every fairy who signed up.

"Come on," Raina said, pulling her friends along. She had read about Tula in her books, and she was anxious to meet her. She was a Gummy Fairy too. But now she lived in the castle with Princess Lolli.

Raina couldn't wait to tell Tula about her new

berries. She hoped she'd like them. And that she could win Tula's vote for the best candy at Candy Fair.

As Raina got closer to the sign-up table, her wings started to flutter. She was so nervous! She had been dreaming of creating a new candy for the fair for so long. And now she was going to present her candy idea. She couldn't believe this was actually happening.

"Name?" Tula asked. She didn't even look up from the large scroll in front of her. In her hand was a large feather that she dipped in a small tub of red syrup for ink.

Raina looked over at her two friends. They pushed her forward toward the table. But Raina was too nervous to speak.

"I'll go first," Cocoa said. She stepped in front

of Raina. "My name is Cocoa the Chocolate Fairy, and this is my friend Melli the Caramel Fairy. We'd like to make chocolate-caramel lollipops."

"We're calling them friendship pops," Melli added.

Tula wrote down the entry on the scroll with her feather pen. "Very well," she said. "Nice to see you working together."

"Thank you," Melli said, smiling.

"Good luck," Tula said. Then she looked up at Raina. "Next?"

"My name is Raina," she said quietly. "I am a Gummy Fairy." She felt her heart beating quickly and her wings fluttering. She had to will herself to stay firmly on the ground as she spoke.

"What will you be presenting at Candy Fair

this year?" Tula asked. She peered over her sparkly glasses.

Raina noticed that there were tiny speckles of sugar crystals along the frames of Tula's glasses. The older fairy also wore a thick, woven red licorice bracelet on her right wrist. Her white hair was swept up in a fancy swirl on the top of her head, and her red dress sparkled in the sun. She was beautiful.

"Sweetie, do you have a candy idea?" Tula asked gently. Her deep blue eyes were kind, and she smiled warmly at Raina.

Immediately Raina felt better. "I'd like to introduce a new gummy candy," she said. Suddenly she had a burst of confidence as she thought of her candy project.

Tula pushed her glasses up on her nose.

"A new gummy candy?" she said. She looked right into Raina's dark eyes. "Very nice. What is the candy called?" She held the feather next to the scroll.

Raina didn't know what to say! She hadn't thought of a name for her candy!

Cocoa leaned in close to them. "They are yummy gummy berries," she said, smiling at Raina. "Each berry is a different color and flavor."

Tula nodded her head. "I see," she said. With careful strokes, she wrote the entry next to Raina's name in fancy script. "That sounds challenging," she added.

"I've done lots of research," Raina explained. "I have everything all planned out. In my garden each berry bush is a different flavor.

The berries will be just perfect."

The older fairy shook her head. "Oh, Raina," she said. "The best candy is not always perfect."

"What do you mean?" Raina asked. She had followed all the rules and had carefully planted the bushes. She was taking excellent care of the plants. She was certain that no Gummy Fairy had ever tried to grow berries like the ones she had. They would be perfect.

"Sometimes the greatest surprises come from the most unlikely places," Tula advised. She smiled at the three fairies standing in front of her. "Good luck with your berries," she said with a wink.

"What do you think she meant?" Raina asked Cocoa and Melli as they flew through the Royal Gardens.

"I'm not sure," Melli said. "But I'm looking forward to the fair. Look at all these fairies here for the sign-up!" She pointed to the long line that snaked through the castle gates.

"Competition will be tough," Cocoa said. A smile spread across her face. "I can't wait!"

"Me neither," Raina gushed. She felt happy after officially signing up for the fair. Now more than ever she wanted to prove that a Gummy Fairy could win the first-place prize at Candy Fair.

CHAPTER 5

Bitter Words

Early the next morning Raina checked on her berry patch. She carefully watered the berry bushes and pruned the leaves. A little gummy bunny poked her head up from underneath one of the bushes.

"Hello," Raina said. She knelt down and scooped up the little bunny with her hand. "What

do you think about these new berries, huh?" She stroked her orange head. "I know you want a bite, but these fruits are for Candy Fair," she told the bunny, "not for you." She carefully placed the bunny outside the fence. Then she plucked a bright purple leaf from another bush for the bunny to nibble on.

Raina closed the fence gate and looked over at the small gummy berry bushes.

Everything looks perfect, she thought happily.

Now that she had signed up for the fair, her plan was moving forward. She had a chance to win the sugar medal this year. She was sure her perfect plan was going to work!

Raina arrived at Chocolate River anxious to tell Berry and Dash about what had happened at Candy Castle. The sugar sand beach along

Chocolate River was their morning meeting spot. The friends tried to meet there every morning to share stories.

When Raina arrived, she was surprised to find Berry already on the sugar beach. The Fruit Fairy was leaning on a large candy rock and making a candy-chew necklace. By her side was a basket filled with sugarcoated jewels. The candies sparkled in the bright morning sun.

As Raina got closer, she saw that Melli and Cocoa were sitting next to Berry. They seemed to be involved in a very serious conversation. Her friends didn't even look up to see that she had flown in.

"Aren't you concerned about Raina?" Berry asked. "All she is talking about is Candy Fair."

"You mean *winning* the sugar medal *at* Candy

Fair," Cocoa corrected her. "I've never seen Raina so focused on something . . . that wasn't a book!"

"I know," Berry said. "I'm concerned about her."

Raina's wings drooped. While she knew that she shouldn't be listening to her friends' conversation, she was hurt that they were talking about her. She stepped out in front of them.

"If you don't think I can win, you should just tell me," Raina stated.

Her three friends all looked up. Berry looked startled. "I didn't see you, Raina," she said, moving closer to her. "I didn't mean that you can't win," she explained. "I'm just worried about you. All you seem focused on is winning the medal. What about enjoying the fair?"

 52

Raina couldn't believe her ears. She flapped her wings and lifted herself up. "I'm leaving," she said. "I have to go over to Red Licorice Lake for some flavor crystals. Since Candy Fair isn't important to you, you wouldn't understand."

Berry looked to Melli and Cocoa. Raina knew her words were bitter, but she couldn't help feeling mad. Winning was important to her—very important.

"Wait," Berry pleaded.

But Raina had already flown off. She sped past Dash as she flew toward Red Licorice Lake.

Dash looked after her, confused. What had she missed?

"I've never seen Raina have such a sugar fit," Cocoa remarked, shaking her head.

"Where was she off to?" Dash asked. She

53

looked after her friend speeding away. "There's a terrible storm coming. All the sugar flies are buzzing about the high winds and rains."

Raina didn't look back. She didn't want to hear a weather report. She was on a mission. Her bushes needed more flavor crystals right away. Her friends just didn't understand. They weren't taking Candy Fair seriously at all! She'd show them who could win first place!

As Raina flew, she saw dark clouds moving quickly toward her. A tiny sugar fly buzzed around her ear, warning her of a dangerous storm. But Raina pressed on.

If I can just get the crystals quickly, she thought, *I'll make it back to Gummy Forest before the rains come!*

A few cool raindrops splashed her face. Raina flew faster. But then the sky turned a

 54

dark purple—a shade she had never seen.

"Head home," a sugar fly buzzed in her ear. "A terrible storm is coming."

Raina swatted the fly away and swooped down to the shore of Red Licorice Lake. As her feet touched the ground, the rain began to fall harder.

She had never seen so much rain! She took out a bottle and scooped up the flavor sprinkles for the berry bushes.

Then a strong gust of wind lifted Raina's feet off the ground. She was picked up and tossed into the air. She sailed across the lake and landed in a sticky web of licorice stalks. Her wings were caught in a tangle of licorice. She couldn't move. She was stuck!

Oh no, she thought.

As much as she tried, her wings wouldn't budge. She couldn't move. As she looked around at the storm whirling around her, she thought about her berry bushes.

I need to get home and protect them, she thought.

The more she struggled to free herself, the more she felt the pull on her wings.

Watching the rain beat down around her, Raina thought about how she had not prepared for the storm. She had not even put a cover over the bushes. Sure as sugar, those bushes would be destroyed.

All her hard work was going to be swirled away by the storm. Her eyes filled with tears.

"How did I let myself get into this sticky mess?" she wailed.

But no one was around to hear her. It seemed that all the other Candy Fairies had listened to the warnings the fruit flies were spreading. And now her perfect candy was going to be ruined. All her dreams of winning the sugar medal were washed away.

 57

6

A Sour Sight

Raina was miserable. She was soaking wet and still stuck in a sticky tangle of licorice vines.

Sure as sugar, my candy berry bushes are destroyed by now, she thought sadly.

As she tried to wiggle free from the vines, Raina thought back over the past couple of weeks. Maybe her friends had been right. She had been so stuck on getting the sugar medal, she wasn't seeing straight. Raina knew she should have listened to the fruit flies. If she had listened, maybe she could have saved her candy . . . and not gotten stuck!

"Raina!" Berry called. The Fruit Fairy appeared before her. She was holding a large lollipop umbrella. "Are you hurt?"

"Not hurt," Raina said. "But I'm stuck." She shielded her eyes from the rain so she could see. "What are you doing here?"

"I knew you wouldn't turn around," Berry said. "Even in this awful storm. I came to see if you were all right." She quickly flew up to Raina and untangled her wings from the sticky red stalks. "I'm sorry about what happened

before at Chocolate River," Berry said. "I was just very worried about you."

Raina fluttered her wings and ducked under Berry's umbrella. "I'm sorry too. You were right, you know," she said. "Winning is all I have been thinking about. And I wouldn't listen to anyone." She looked down at her wet dress. "Now all my chances are ruined."

"You don't know that for sure," Berry said. "Come on, let's head back to the forest. Maybe the bushes are fine."

Raina hugged her friend. She was so thankful for her bravery—and her friendship. Berry was a special kind of friend—the *best* kind.

Together, the two fairies flew off into the storm, careful of falling branches and pelting rain.

"What a gooey mess!" Raina cried as she flew over Gummy Forest. The storm had hit the forest hard. Many of the trees were down, and most of the crops looked destroyed. Raina always kept the forest orderly and clean. This was a very sour sight indeed.

As the two fairies landed, the rain began to stop. But the damage was already done.

"Oh no!" Raina cried. Her heart sank as she saw so many of the gummy animals wandering around. They all looked lost. Suddenly her candy for the fair didn't seem as important as helping the animals rebuild their homes.

"Come on, Berry," Raina said, zooming down into the forest. "We have to help."

Berry was right behind her. Her heart ached

when she saw all the sad animals—especially the gummy cubs.

Raina sprang into action. She organized the gummy bears in a line and set up a food station for them. She rounded up the gummy birds, keeping them together. "We'll get this mess sorted out in no time," she told the flock. "Don't worry. We'll get your homes back in order right away."

All the animals listened to Raina as she calmly began the cleanup. She was able to make all the animals feel secure and safe.

Raina bent down to pet a little blue gummy cub. "Don't worry, Blue Belle," she said, smiling. "You'll be just fine."

As Berry watched Raina work, she beamed with pride. Raina was a talented Candy Fairy and her candy was spectacular, but her true talent was working with the gummy animals. She knew that seeing Gummy Forest in such a mess was upsetting to Raina, but the Gummy Fairy didn't let that show. She was concentrating on helping the animals.

A small gummy bunny hopped up to Raina. He nuzzled his nose into her leg. "I know," Raina said, petting his head. "I promise that you'll be back in your bunny hole by nighttime."

Raina looked around the messy forest and sighed. If only she could find the hole under all the fallen leaves and branches!

Just then Raina looked up to see her friends Cocoa, Melli, and Dash. Their wings were still wet from the strong rains.

"We're here to help," Cocoa said. "We knew you'd need some extra fairy power."

Raina smiled. She had never been so happy to see her friends! She knew what a great sacrifice they had each made to come to Gummy Forest.

"We knew you'd be upset," Cocoa told her.

"And we wanted to help," Melli said.

"We can get this cleaned up in no time," Dash added.

Raina stared at her friends. They had braved the storm to come help her. She reached out and hugged them. "Thank you," she said. "It's so important that we clean up the branches so that the animals can get back to their homes before nighttime. Will you help?"

"Of course!" Melli exclaimed. "You tell us what to do. Sure as sugar, if we work together, we can clean the forest up by nightfall."

The fairies worked quickly and followed all of Raina's directions. Together, the five friends carried fallen branches, picked up leaves, and uncovered nests. They rebuilt a few homes for the animals and replanted a couple of trees. Very soon the forest was back to normal.

"Here you go," Raina said. She grinned as she placed a young gummy bird back in her nest. "I bet you need a good rest after that storm." She smiled at the bird and then flew back down to the ground.

"Are you ready to head over to Gummy Lake?" Berry asked. Now that all the animals

were safe, she knew Raina would be curious about her berry bushes.

"We'll go with you," Melli told her.

The fairies all gathered around Raina.

"Thanks," Raina whispered. She looked around at her friends. "I'm sorry that I've been so stuck on Candy Fair." She wiped a tear from her eye. "I can't believe that it took a big storm to see clearly."

"Don't start crying," Berry said, smiling. "There's been enough water in this forest already today! Besides, don't you want to see what happened to the berry bushes?"

The five fairies flew to Gummy Lake. When they arrived, Raina saw her berry garden and gasped.

The storm had destroyed the bushes. The branches were broken and the berries were flattened. Just as she had expected, her prized gummy berries were ruined.

CHAPTER 7

A Berry Surprise

Raina sat down at the edge of her berry garden. She peered at the berry bushes. She couldn't believe the sight. Her heart sank as she gazed at the fruit dangling from the branches. Each berry was not only flat, but a swirl of different colors. No longer were there red, blue, yellow, orange, green, and purple berries hanging from the branches. They were all rainbow swirled!

"Oh, sugar sticks!" Raina cried. "Who has ever seen candy quite like this! This is a disaster! I'll have nothing to show at Candy Fair tomorrow."

"The rain must have swirled the colors together," Melli said. She leaned in closer to get

a better view. "You're right. I've never seen any candy like that."

Plucking a berry from the vine, Raina lifted the rainbow-colored candy. She held it up to her friends. "All I could think about were these berries, and now look at them. What kind of Gummy Fairy am I? I should have been home trying to protect the bushes instead of trying to make them even better."

"Oh, Raina," Berry gushed. "You are the kindest Gummy Fairy. Without you, the gummy animals would have been lost and without homes. You were the one who organized the forest clean-up." She took a step closer and plucked the berry from Raina's hand. She held it up to the sun. Carefully, she examined the colorful candy. "Besides, I don't think these berries are ruined," she said.

"What do you think it tastes like?" Dash asked. When she saw the stern looks on her friends' faces, she shrugged. "What? I'm just asking!"

"Dash is right," Berry said. "Maybe the berries taste even better."

Raina shook her head. "Not likely," she said. "Look at them!" She sank down to the soggy, wet ground. "My perfect candy is now a swirl of a mess. I'm sure the flavors are a swirled mess too."

Melli stepped forward. "Don't you remember what Tula said? She said that sometimes the greatest surprises make the sweetest candy."

"She did say that," Cocoa confirmed. "Dash is right. Maybe we should taste the berries."

Berry picked another berry from the branch. "The candy does look beautiful," she said with a smile. "I have a tie-dye rainbow skirt that looks similar," she said. "Rainbow tie-dye is definitely very fashionable."

Rolling her eyes, Raina sighed. "But rainbow candy?" she said, full of doubt. "Whoever heard of such a gummy thing?"

"That's the point!" Berry replied. "Come on, taste it, Raina. If anyone can make a rainbow taste good, it would be you. You were born on the day the Great Rainbow appeared!"

Berry did have a point. Raina took a bite of the rainbow berry.

"How does it taste?" Cocoa asked, leaning closer to her.

"It tastes . . . ," Raina said as she chewed, "delicious!" A wide smile appeared on her face. "Lickin' lollipops, I did it!" she cried. Her wings fluttered and she shot straight up in the air. After a quick turn, Raina landed next to the bush and took another candy. She popped the berry in her mouth.

The flavors are a terrific blend, she thought. *Sweet, tangy, and juicy!*

Raina handed a berry to each of her friends.

"It's a rainbow fruit bowl," Melli declared. She licked her fingers and smiled.

"Congratulations," Dash said.

"*Gumm-er-ific!*" Cocoa added, laughing.

"You see, there is a rainbow after every storm," Berry told her. She gave Raina a tight hug. "And you've just discovered the secret of the rainbow! It's gummy yummy."

"I couldn't have done it without all of you," Raina said. She looked around at her friends with a serious expression. "Thank you."

"For what?" Dash asked. She reached out for another rainbow swirl berry.

"For believing in me," Raina said. "And for helping me clear out the forest. You are the sweetest friends a fairy could ever have. Thank you."

They all shared a group hug, and then they picked the berries for Candy Fair. Suddenly Raina had her competitive spirit back. She was ready to go to Candy Fair with her new swirled candy. So what if the candy wasn't perfect—it was perfectly her own. And Raina wanted to share the berries with everyone in Sugar Valley.

CHAPTER 8

Candy Fair

The next morning, the caramel trumpets blew as the royal gates of the castle opened. Candy Fair had officially begun! The Royal Gardens were filled with small white tents, all brimming with candy from Sugar Valley. Rows of tables were set up with Candy Fairies showing their new sweet treats. Some fairies had decorated their booths with candy, and some had fancy stands and signs to showcase their treats. There were old favorites like chocolates, jelly beans, and lollipops. But there were also more elaborate and new candies for the fairies of Sugar Valley to taste.

There was excitement in the air with so many new and delicious treats. Candy Fair was a very special day in the kingdom.

The storm had hit Gummy Forest the hardest, so other candies seemed to have been unharmed by the rain. After the storm the day turned out to be a beautiful and clear spring day.

Cocoa and Melli were at the booth next to Raina's, showing their chocolate-caramel lollipops. The caramel was swirled on a stick like whipped cream on an ice cream sundae. Carefully, Cocoa and Melli had dipped each caramel pop in dark chocolate and dusted the pops with colored sprinkles. Melli had stuck the lollipops into a sugar pinecone, so the pops were displayed beautifully in tiers. Many fairies were lined up to sample the candy.

"Yum!" Dash exclaimed. She reached for another one from the table.

"Hold on," Cocoa said. She stopped Dash's hand before she could touch another pop. "We have to save some for the judges."

"I know," Dash said. She flashed Cocoa a sly smile. "How about just one more?"

Melli slipped Dash another pop. "Last one, okay?" she said. It was hard for her to say no to her friend.

"Thanks, Melli," Dash told her. She took a bite out of the tasty pop. "Sure as sugar, these are the best pops you've ever made."

Raina was happy to see the line of fairies at her booth. Word had spread quickly around the fair that Raina had a new gummy candy. Many of the fairies were curious to see the candy that had survived the rainstorm. And to find out what made Raina's candy so different.

As she handed out her berries to the fairies, Raina heard only good reviews. But Raina knew that the judges were the ones to have the final say on who got the sugar medal. She searched the crowds for Princess Lolli and her advisers.

She was growing a bit concerned. If Princess Lolli didn't come soon, all her berries would be gone! She didn't want to turn away any fairy, but she had to save some for the judges.

When Tula appeared before her, Raina gasped. Seeing one of the judges at her table made her nervous. She knocked over two baskets of her berries! Quickly, she scrambled to pick up the candies. When she stood up, Tula was waiting for her.

"Hello again," Tula said calmly. She pushed her sparkling glasses up on her nose. "Is this the new gummy berry that you told me about at the sign-up?" She held up a berry to take a closer look.

"Not exactly," Raina said. "The candy turned

out a little differently than I had planned."

Tula picked up the rainbow berry and took a bite. "Hmm," she said as she chewed. "How did you get the colors to swirl?"

"The colors just appeared on the berries after the storm—just like a rainbow," Raina said, smiling. "And they are filled with the sweetness of the rain clearing after a storm."

"Very interesting," Tula said. She examined the multicolored berry in her hand. "Different."

"I know that they're not the *perfect* berry," Raina said, hanging her head. Suddenly she felt embarrassed about her less-than-perfect berries. The more Tula examined her candy, the more nervous she became. Slowly, she raised her head. She watched Tula's expression as the Royal Fairy finished eating the candy.

"Ah, but they are *perfectly* sweet," Tula said. She lifted her glasses and peered down at Raina. "Well done, Raina."

"Thank you," Raina said. She thought she was going to burst with pride. "I wouldn't have thought of showing this candy if it weren't for my friends," she added. "They gave me the courage to see that something not perfect might actually be better than planned."

"Yes, friends make life sweeter, that is for sure," Tula said. "And so do acts of kindness." She took off her glasses and looked Raina directly in the eyes. "I heard how you and your friends cleaned up the forest for the gummy animals after the storm yesterday."

"Yes," Raina said. "The forest was quite a mess after all that rain and wind."

 85

"You are a kind and good fairy," Tula said. "And your candy is delicious. Thank you for sharing this candy here today."

Raina couldn't respond. She was too excited. Tula liked her candy! Maybe her dream of getting the sugar medal was going to happen! Raina crossed her fingers for good luck as she watched Tula fly off to the next tent.

"May I try one of your berries?" a small Gummy Fairy asked.

Raina turned her attention back to the line of fairies in front of her table. She smiled at the little fairy and handed her a berry.

"Enjoy," she said.

Holding her hand up to her eyes, Raina shielded the sun from her face and looked around the gardens. Where was Princess Lolli? She hoped the fairy princess and the other two advisers would come soon. The suspense of finding out who would win the sugar medal was growing—and Raina couldn't wait anymore!

Looking up at the sky, she saw the large sun above. Once the sun began to move toward the Frosted Mountains, the judges would have to submit their final decisions. Raina didn't think she could wait till Sun Dip today!

The awards ceremony would start once the sun began to slide behind the mountains. Raina felt as if the day was moving slower than any other day. Everyone in Sugar Valley was eager to hear who would win the sugar medal!

CHAPTER 9

Tasty Tastings

Jumping jelly beans!" Berry cried when she saw Raina. She had been flying around the Royal Gardens looking for her friend. There were so many booths set up in the gardens that it took her a long time to find Raina and her booth with the rainbow gummy berries. "Raina, you have the longest line for candy here at the fair." Berry pointed to the line of fairies waiting patiently for their candy.

"I know!" Raina said, working quickly. She was busy handing out her berries, but careful to leave a special basket off to the side. When Princess Lolli finally came, Raina wanted to make sure she had candy for her to sample.

"I'll help you," Berry offered. She landed next to Raina and started to hand out the rainbow candies. "Try a yummy gummy berry!" she called out.

Raina smiled. Berry's enthusiasm was making everyone excited about the new candy. She was thrilled that Berry had come to the fair.

"Thank you for coming today," Raina told her.

"I wouldn't have missed it!" she cried. "Just because I didn't want to show my own candy didn't mean I wouldn't be here for you."

Raina gave Berry a tight hug. "Thank you."

As she pulled away from her friend, she noticed a little Chocolate Fairy staring at Berry's necklace.

"I love your necklace," the little fairy said to Berry.

Blushing, Berry smiled. "Thanks," she said. "I made it out of fresh fruit chews."

"Sugar snaps," the fairy cheered. "I'd love one. Could you make one for me?"

"Sure," Berry replied, grinning.

"I told you other fairies would love the jewelry!" Raina said, giving Berry a nudge.

"You might be on to something," Berry agreed. "I have gotten a few comments on the necklace today." She put her arm around Raina. "But today is about sweet candy—and the sugar medal. Has Princess Lolli been here yet?"

"No," Raina said, shaking her head. She was beginning to wonder if the princess would ever come sample her candy. She didn't have time to fret, though. There were too many fairies wanting to try her rainbow candies. As she spoke, she continued to pass out her yummy gummy berries. All the fairies seemed to be enjoying the treat, and Raina was so pleased.

"What if I run out before Princess Lolli gets here?" Raina whispered to Berry.

At that very moment Princess Lolli stepped

up to Raina's table. With her were two Royal Fairies. They were ready to judge her candy!

"What do we have here?" the fairy princess asked. She gave Raina a warm smile. Her beautiful long pink dress flowed out behind her. "These look gorgeous. May I have one, please?"

"Oh, yes, of course!" Raina exclaimed. She handed a rainbow berry to the fairy princess.

Holding her breath, Raina tried to wait patiently as Princess Lolli tasted her candy. The princess fixed her candy tiara on top of her long strawberry-blond hair.

"Very good, Raina," she declared. "This year it seems there are so many new candies. I think we have some tough decisions to make." The princess turned to her two advisers and handed them each a berry.

Raina stood still as a sugar cube. She wasn't sure what to say to the princess!

"We will be announcing the awards soon," Princess Lolli said. "Raina, these berries were a very sweet treat."

As the fairy princess spoke, the two advisers scribbled notes on a large parchment scroll.

Raina was so curious about what the two advisers wrote! She had to wonder if they liked the different berries, and if they thought they were worthy of the sugar medal.

"Everyone has done a great job!" the princess exclaimed. "Even with the terrible storm. This will be a very difficult decision for us to make. Thank you, Raina, and good luck!"

The fairy princess flew off to another tent with her two advisers by her side. She still had

more tastings to do before Sun Dip.

Raina sighed. She leaned on the table in front of her.

"Don't worry," Berry whispered. She stood close to her friend and squeezed her shoulder. "I think Princess Lolli liked the berry very much."

"Do you really think so?" Raina asked. "Maybe she is saying those nice things to all the fairies who made candy."

"I don't think so," Berry said, shaking her head.

Raina wasn't sure what Princess Lolli was thinking. She was only sure that she would find waiting for the awards ceremony very difficult!

CHAPTER 10

The Sweetest Award

Finally the caramel horns blew again, announcing that the awards ceremony would begin shortly. All the fairies moved to the center of the gardens, where a stage was set up. Princess Lolli, Tula, and three other Royal Fairies were sitting on royal chairs on the stage. Princess Lolli was in the middle, sitting in her candy throne bedazzled with crystal candy jewels.

"Welcome to Candy Fair!" Princess Lolli said to the large crowd of fairies. "This year was an extraordinarily sweet year. A big fairy thank-you to all the fairies who prepared so many candy treats." She turned to smile at the advisers behind her. "We had a very difficult decision to make. There were many, many worthy candies this year."

Raina held Berry's hand. Standing around them were Melli, Cocoa, and Dash. At that moment Raina was happy to have her friends near. Without them, this moment would not have been as special.

Dash moaned and rubbed her belly. "I think I ate too much candy today," she said. "Princess Lolli is right. Everything was so yummy. I couldn't stop myself!"

"That's why Candy Fair is every four years, not every year," Berry said with a grin.

"And now for the moment we've all been waiting for," Princess Lolli said. She looked around at the crowd, smiling. "I am pleased to present this year's sugar medal to . . ."

Everyone was quiet. Raina closed her eyes and squeezed Berry's and Melli's hands.

"The winner of the sugar medal is," Princess Lolli announced, "Miro the Gummy Fairy for her beautiful and tasty gummy flowers!"

A roar of applause erupted. Raina turned to see Miro. She was grinning as she flew up to the stage to get her medal.

Though Raina felt disappointed, she was proud of Miro. The young fairy had listened to the fruit flies' warnings and taken good care of her crops during the storm. She deserved praise for her fine gummy candy. Raina was very happy that for the first time ever a Gummy Fairy had won the medal.

She felt Berry squeeze her hand. She squeezed Berry's hand back, thankful again that her friends were by her side.

"And finally," Princess Lolli said. She put her hands up to quiet the crowd. "There is one more award this year."

A hush came over the crowd of fairies.

"It is not often that this award is given," Princess Lolli said. "And I am especially proud to award this to a very special fairy."

"What is this about?" Raina whispered to Berry. She had no idea what the princess was talking about. The sugar medal was the first prize. What other award could there be? She had never read about another award in any of her books. Sure, there were honorable mentions, but another award?

Berry shrugged and looked back to the fairy princess.

Everyone was eager to hear what the princess had to say.

"I would like to award the great honor of the pink candy heart to Raina the Gummy Fairy," Princess Lolli proclaimed. "The special pink candy heart is for her dedication to the animals in Gummy Forest. On behalf of the entire Candy Kingdom, and all of Sugar Valley," the princess said, "we thank you for your hard work. The animals would not have had a place to stay after the storm if it hadn't been for your quick thinking and dedication."

All the fairies in the Royal Gardens cheered wildly. The Gummy Fairies were the loudest. Raina gave a small wave, blushing. She didn't win the sugar medal, but the pink candy heart was a thrilling surprise. As Princess Lolli said, the pink candy heart was not given often, and it was a true treasure.

She looked over and saw Tula smiling at her.

"This will go down in the books as a very special day for all the Gummy Fairies," Princess Lolli continued. "And for all Candy Fairies everywhere."

"Well, go get your award," Berry said, nudging Raina toward the stage.

101

Raina looked at her friends. "You all need to come with me. We all worked together that day, and you deserve the honor too."

The five fairies held hands and flew up to the stage. Princess Lolli pinned the sugar crystal pink heart on Raina's dress.

"I'm very proud of you," the fairy princess told her. "And those rainbow gummy berries were delicious!" She leaned in closer. "Do you think we can grow more of them?"

"Sure as sugar!" Raina blurted out.

"I'm glad," Princess Lolli said. "Thank you, Raina."

Raina took in all the praise, and then looked up at the princess. "Thank you, Princess Lolli," Raina said. Then she grabbed her friends and brought them onstage with her. "But I wouldn't

have been able to do anything without my friends.
They were a great help. I want to share this award
with them."

The loud cheers from the Royal Gardens
swept up high into the Frosted Mountains. Raina
beamed with pride.

"You look great with that candy heart," Berry

said, smiling at her friend. "Well deserved!"

"And it's so sparkly and shiny!" Dash remarked.

"It is special," Melli said.

"Congratulations!" Cocoa added.

"Thank you," Raina said. She hugged her friends. "This was a sweet surprise. And I'll treasure this award forever . . . just like I treasure all of you!"

Raina's candy hadn't turned out as she planned, and Candy Fair did not go as expected. But she couldn't have been happier. Indeed, the sweetest events are not always the ones planned. And they are made even sweeter when surrounded by good, true friends.

FIND OUT

WHAT HAPPENS IN

The caramel stalks on the hill glowed golden in the late afternoon sun. Melli, a Caramel Fairy, took a deep breath. She smelled the sweet, sugary scent of fresh caramel. Sitting on a branch of a chocolate oak, she gave a heavy sigh. It was nice to relax after a day's work in the fields.

From the tree she could see out to Caramel

Hills and Candy Corn Fields. This was one of her favorite spots in Sugar Valley. A gentle breeze blew her short, dark hair. The cool air reminded her that the weather was turning colder. While she was sorry that the long, sunny days of summer were over, Melli loved the change of season.

Autumn was the busiest time of year for the Caramel Fairies. Many of their candies were grown and harvested in the autumn months. And Melli's favorite was candy corn. Not only did she love the sweet treat, she loved the Caramel Moon Festival, too.

This event, the best event of the fall, was held during the evening of the full moon in the tenth month of the year. Princess Lolli, the ruling fairy princess of Candy Kingdom, officially named that moon Caramel Moon. The candy corn was at the peak of perfection at that time, and the candy crops needed to be picked when they were ripe, so all the fairies in Sugar Valley came to help. The festival was a giant party with lots of candy corn, music, and dancing.

"Hi, Melli!" Cara called out. Cara was Melli's little sister. She flew up and sat on the branch beside Melli.

"Hey, Cara," Melli said. "How'd you find me?"

"I knew you'd be here," Cara told her. "It's almost Sun Dip and you always wait for Cocoa here."

Melli laughed. Her little sister was right. The chocolate oak at the bottom of Caramel Hill was at the edge of Chocolate Woods. The old tree was the perfect meeting spot for Melli and her best friend, Cocoa the Chocolate Fairy. They always flew together to see their friends at the end of the day when the sun dipped below the Frosted Mountains. Sun Dip was a time for meeting friends and sharing candy and news of the day.

"I just heard some golden news," Cara went on. A smile spread across her face. "You'll never guess who is playing at the Caramel Moon Festival this year!" Her lavender wings fluttered so fast that she flew up off the branch.

"You found out who is playing?" Melli asked. Her dark eyes sparkled with excitement.

All year long, fairies tried to guess who would play the music at the late-night celebration. After the candy corn was picked, all the fairies celebrated by the light of the moon. Good music was a key ingredient to making the party a success.

Since this year Melli was old enough to have planted the seeds in the fields and stay late to help pick the candy corn, she was even more excited about the music at the festival.

Cara grinned at Melli. She usually didn't hear juicy information before her older sister. Melli wanted to savor the sweet moment of knowing something before Melli.

"Come on," Melli urged. "Please tell me! I want to know!" She grabbed Cara's hand.

"Well, it's your favorite band," Cara said. She looked as if she would burst with excitement.

Melli's mouth fell open. "The Sugar Pops are coming here?" Her purple wings began to flutter, and her heart began to beat faster. "Are you serious?"

"Sure as sugar," Cara said. "I was at Candy

Castle to make a delivery and I heard the Royal Fairies talking about the Caramel Moon Festival. The Sugar Pops are really coming!"

The Sugar Pops were the greatest band in the entire kingdom. Their music was fun to dance to and Melli knew every single song by heart. She also knew everything about Chip, Char, and Carob Pop. The three Pop brothers sang *and* played instruments. They had the sweetest songs and were the most popular band in Sugar Valley.

"Hot caramel!" Melli exclaimed. "Wait until I tell everyone at Sun Dip!" She reached out and hugged her sister. "Thanks for telling me, Cara. This is fantastic news." Her mind was racing. "If they sing 'Yum Pop,' I will melt!"

Cara nodded. "Oh, they have to play that

song!" she exclaimed. "It's their best one." She smiled.

Melli looked toward Chocolate Woods. She kept an eye out for Cocoa. Cocoa loved the Sugar Pops too. Actually, all her friends did. And this year they would be able to stay and help harvest the crops, which meant they'd also get to see the Sugar Pops perform.

"What about me? Do you think I can see the Sugar Pops?" Cara asked.

"I'll see if I can get you permission," Melli said. She leaned in closer to Cara and put her arm around her. She didn't want to see her sister so sad. "Maybe you can come for one or two songs."

"Thanks, Melli," Cara said. Her wings perked up a little at the possibility of seeing the band play.

Just at that moment, Cocoa flew up to the chocolate oak. "Hello fairies!" she called out. "What's new and delicious?"

Melli and Cara both grinned.

"What?" Cocoa asked. She looked at the two sisters. "What are you up to?"

Melli's wings flapped and she floated off the branch. She couldn't contain her excitement! "Cara found out that the Sugar Pops are playing at Caramel Moon Festival!" she burst out.

Cocoa clapped her hands together. *"Choc-o-rific!"* she shouted. "That is the sweetest news I've heard all day!" She sat down on one of the chocolate oak's branches. "Wait until the others hear about this. And this year we'll get to stay the whole night!"

Melli nudged Cocoa. She knew that Cara was feeling sad about not being old enough to stay for the night concert. "We're going to see if Cara can come for at least one song," she told Cocoa.

"'Yum Pop,' I hope," Cara said. She held up crossed fingers.

Melli and Cocoa laughed.

"Come on," Cocoa said. "Let's head over to Sun Dip and tell the others."

"I want to go check on the candy corn crops before Sun Dip," Melli said. "All the Caramel Fairies were working on Caramel Hill today. I haven't been since yesterday. I'll meet you at Red Licorice Lake."

Melli gave quick hugs to Cara and Cocoa.

"I'll see you later," Cara called as she flew back home to Caramel Hill.

"See you soon, Cara," Cocoa said. "And, Melli, bring some of your caramel!"

"Of course!" Melli called. She still had a smile on her face as she flew toward the fields.

The Caramel Moon Festival was bound to be the most extraordinary event of the year!